Towards the Sun

An Anthology for Chloe

Dedicated to Chloe Dean and her positive bravery

With thanks to all artists and authors who contributed to this book

And to all who have donated to help Chloe's fight… including you, reader

Foreword

By T. M. Lowe

What is hope? The Merriam-Webster dictionary defines it in two ways, each with a slightly different feel and nuance. The first definition states that hope is "to cherish a desire with anticipation; to want something to happen or be true". This is passive - hoping that a good outcome occurs. The second definition is a little more active: "desire accompanied by expectation of or belief in fulfillment". This is still hoping that a good outcome occurs, but there is also an underlying sense that it *will* happen. Faith. Belief. Perhaps, even, superstition that one can will into existence certain outcomes through hard work, perseverance, an attitude that refuses to give up or give in even when life is at its darkest, all driven by hope.

It is that second definition and all the underlying ripples of nuance that define the hopepunk genre of writing. It stands against the brutal negativity (some would argue "realism") of grimdark. Some may view it as cliché. Some may argue that there are no true happy endings, that such fantasies are best left to childhood movies or stories where good defeats evil and everyone lives happily ever after. But, at its core, hopepunk isn't about shedding realism for an impossible fantasy; it's about rising up and fighting, in spite of everything bad and dark, with a belief and hope that fighting the good fight will do some good, have some positive impact, and maybe - just maybe - win the day in the end.

A living embodiment of that hope is Chloe Dean, for whom this book was created. In February 2020, just before COVID-19 plunged the world into a state of fear, this 19-year-old St. Augustine, Florida artist was diagnosed with an exceedingly rare liver cancer: Fibrolamellar Carcinoma. It affects teens and young adults with otherwise healthy livers and is so rare that it makes up only one to five percent of all liver cancers. Despite the grim diagnosis, Chloe has faced it as merely a challenge to fight and overcome, powered by her own inner positivity and hope.

To help her and her family with the medical expenses, as well as the travel expenses for being treated by an out-of-state specialist, a GoFundMe was launched to help fundraise for Chloe's battle. This anthology of hopepunk-themed prose, poetry, and artwork is the final piece in our efforts to spread Chloe's story and boundless, hopeful optimism – 100% of all sales of this book, digital and print, will be donated to her GoFundMe at https://www.gofundme.com/f/help-chloe-be-cancerfree

When the night is at its darkest, hope is what keeps you going until the dawn. For every night has an end, and every day has a new beginning with new potential. Turn your back on the shadows of the night as they fall away and instead – with hope in your heart and a will to succeed – turn towards the sun.

Thank you for helping support Chloe's fight with your purchase of this compendium. And now, gentle reader, I leave you with one final thought and blessing: may you always aspire, may you always question, and may the wind always be to thy wings.

FIELDS OF JOY

In the fields
Of Torlis
Where the wind
Makes flowers sway

Here gather
Fair folk
And nymphs
Who cherish play

Sounds of bells chiming
Echo sweetly in the air
The laughter of young ones
With flowers in their hair

A plenitude of goods
With the utmost to share
Love set its roots here
There is no place for despair

-Adrienne T. Nugent

SPIRIT ANIMAL

Thank you

My eternal friend

For carrying my sorrow with you

Across the sky

Into a new divide

Compassion rests

Like a burning flame

On the wings of change

Hear the music play

I am intoxicated by your ways

-Deanna Stinson

PREFACE

By Estee Lee-Mountel

Back in 2017, the crew at Advenworks came up with an idea for a cyberpunk runner-slasher game that would combine the best qualities of titles like *Flappy Bird* and *Fruit Ninja*. It was called... well... *Slashrun*. Self-explanatory and straightforward, right? They had a general sense for the art direction and feel of the game but needed my help to breathe a little more life into the universe. 2017 had been rather bleak; we wanted to offer some hope. Randomly, I'd find myself humming that old gospel song, "This Little Light of Mine." The song itself became a pillar of strength during the US Civil Rights Movement of the 50s and 60s as a "freedom song," sung during long marches and protests. It was sung during the counterdemonstration at Charlottesville in 2017. It got me through the rough days and became the inspiration for *Slashrun*'s worldbuilding.

The team decided to forego the reference, however, to keep the game culturally neutral— which I agreed with. In the end, I came up with ~150 words on Ash, our hero, and the universe of *Slashrun*; it had to be kept short due to space restrictions on our Kickstarter. It spoke of a jealous darkness, hellbent on consuming humankind's light due to their brilliance and advancements. If you're a fan of the novel *A Wrinkle in Time*, the imagery may seem familiar. The hero's job was to combat the darkness by hacking and slashing their way through the city and releasing light back into the world. I left it at that; and, honestly, I doubted anyone wanted a novella for a mobile game's backstory.

Fast forward to two weeks ago. We received word that 19-year-old Chloe, daughter of "New Beginnings" cover artist/designer Brook Dean, was diagnosed with a very rare form of liver cancer. The family has a very long road ahead of them, but we're going to help with everything we have: the ability to create. Our theme? *Hope.* Admittedly, I was stuck on story ideas for a while; a lot of my creative energy was being channeled into my work at the public library. Out of the blue, in the midst of my stress, I started singing under my breath, *This little light of mine; I'm gonna let it shine.* It was finally time to give Ash's story and the world of *Slashrun* their due.

Because, if anything, Ash literally runs on the light of hope and little else.

And then fast forward a few more weeks. The entire planet is embroiled in a pandemic. Because, you know, of course it is. I finished this piece as most of us folks in the US were settling in for an extended lockdown due to COVID-19. Going back through the manuscript, I realized how— oh, what's the word... apropos?— this story was: the darkness that seemed to settle over everything and everyone; the fear; the idea that we, the human race, was brought low by something unknown and frightening. Yet the story and the message stay the same, don't they? Whether it's The Darkness; or systemic racial oppression; or a global pandemic, we keep hoping. In the face of uncertainty and immense danger, we cling to hope that tomorrow will bring us something new, something better. Before you even ask: NO, I didn't write the monstrosity that is 2020 so far into existence. At least, I don't think I did. But anyway, back to Ash and the story of *Slashrun*...

When things look bleak and you're facing your darkest hour, remember you always have a light in you— unquenchable, unending, indomitable.

Let it shine.

THIS LITTLE LIGHT OF MINE

By Estee Lee-Mountel

I t's all I have left.

Despite all the rags and assorted detritus I've piled on top of it to hide its existence, the glow of the Lightblade is persistent. Insistent, even. Such a wondrous thing deserved better: better treatment, better handling, and, most of all, better than me. I'm just a nobody who happened to find and bond with one of the world's remaining light artifacts that survived the Arrival. When I first found it, I had no idea what it was nor what I should do with it. Not until The Darkness's shadow minions started converging on me and I started swinging this glowing *thing* I'd just found in a frenzied panic. As each form evaporated under the blade, a small globule of light coalesced from the dissipating shroud and hung in midair for a brief second before zipping away to turn on a nearby streetlight or room. The light was small, almost inconsequential, and barely lasted more than a few minutes. But it was enough to spark something; the idea that I could fight back against The Darkness with the Lightblade's help.

In an ideal world, it would be on display in a museum or on a monument for everyone to admire. Instead, it's stuck going on patrol runs with me around the city. Life has, unfortunately, been anything *but* ideal for the last eight months.

When The Darkness first arrived on Earth, we didn't understand what was happening at first— sudden cloud cover or an eclipse perhaps. We had nothing to fear then; how could we have known we were in danger? Words like "fear" and "danger" were only used in entertainment media to generate cheap thrills. We were living in a shining age of technological and cultural advancement where most of humanity's issues no longer existed. It seemed like we were unstoppable. We felt *invincible*.

Before long, the lights started fading out of existence, one by one. It was slow, almost methodical; like a solitary diner savoring their meal, one morsel at a time. Whole city sectors went dark each day. By the end of the week, all of San Pacifica had reverted to the use of primitive wood fires to provide warmth and light. The only way to tell the passing of days is diligent use of a clock and calendar. There's no sunrise or sunset anymore; no stars nor moon to help us mark time as we had in the days when our people still dwelled in caves.

Within months, Earth had become completely lightless. People had initially tried to continue their lives as normal, but it proved more and more difficult with each passing day. The Darkness hadn't just shown up and consumed the world's light. Even after it was obvious that we had nothing else to give, it stuck around. Waiting. Gloating. Its very existence was palpably oppressive and stifling; a thick, heavy scarf wrapped around your head in the middle of summer.

Some began to whisper that it wanted to consume *us*, too. Rumors ran rampant that so-and-so heard from such-and-such about the disappearance of this-and-that's cousin's neighbor's ex-roommate in college. It was easy to dismiss when they were just that: rumors. Most of us were still negotiating who got to use what at which times and forming queues. Now, it's easy to tell. Streets and homes are emptier; there's less competition for resources. Those who are left scurry about like furtive animals. We eventually figured out whom The Darkness was taking, realizing the pattern too late. It seemed random— a teacher here; a first responder there; that one clerk at the coffeeshop who never loses their cool no matter how busy they are; the librarian who patiently figures out what you mean by "that one book with the blue cover and might've come out a year or two ago maybe"; the kid who always waves hello during your morning commute. They were the best and brightest of us; people with seemingly small gifts we'd always taken for granted.

People like my mother.

I finally roll off the thin mat and stand up, unable to rest— desperately trying to push the dark thoughts back into their appropriate hidey-holes in my mind. Running patrols in the city used to clear my head. It gave me a purpose. Lately, however, it's been difficult to keep the despair at bay. There just doesn't seem to be a point to the patrols anymore. Nothing I did made a difference. We're still under The Darkness with no end in sight. No matter how much light I liberate from the shadow minions, it's not enough.

The glow from the Lightblade flares up as if in response to my wallowing. With a resigned sigh, I unbury it from the pile and pack up my meager camp. It's not like I have anything else on my agenda, right? Might as well go on another trip through the city. It probably won't be much different from the other runs, but at least it's something to do. And, honestly, taking down agents of The Darkness feels good.

I close my eyes, the Lightblade in line with my outstretched arm like a natural extension of my body. As usual, I feel an unseen force tug at my body toward a specific direction. I hate to admit it, but I didn't take up running for my health. At the risk of sounding superstitious or even religious, I'm pretty sure the Lightblade *knows* where to find the shadow minions, itching to fight them; it just needs me to get it there and help it do its work. And when we're in combat, I couldn't tell you where I end, and the blade begins. I've never taken a single lesson in fencing or karate or thrown a punch in my life, mind you; but, with the blade in my hand, it's effortless and easy.

My legs are already moving while I'm in mid-reverie, heading in the direction of the tug I'd felt a moment ago. Our first stop occurs about two miles into the journey when I hear the panicked cry of a child. The Lightblade thrums with a surge of energy as we quickly approach the shadow minion that's currently trying to wrench a woman from the child's grasp. It towers over them. Its face is blank and expressionless, but I can hear the prideful, rasping chuckle that ripples out from its maw. The noise itself is a mockery of laughter and joy. With its prize secured, it starts to turn and move away.

"Mama!" The child's voice is strangled by sobs as he screams for the woman again and again. "MAMA!!"

The shadow minion looks back, laughs derisively, then resumes its journey— only to find itself face to face with me and the Lightblade. Our first cut arcs down into the arm holding the woman. I bring the blade back up in the follow-through, slicing across the torso; and then shear its head right off its shoulders with another swing. As the creature loses its shape and evaporates into the air, three globes of light take form. They gently bob in the space above the tiny family's heads. The woman, cradling her sniffling child, looks up and silently mouths, "Thank you."

I nod to her, scanning the area carefully for more shadow minions. As the light globes float up and reveal what was once a vibrant park and playground, I take off once more. That tug I'd felt earlier is stronger, more insistent this time. Every so often, a shadow minion or two will jump into my path. The Lightblade and I quickly dispatch them, then move on. And each time, before heading back into the dark, I commit each bit of scenery to memory as they're briefly lit up and brought back to life: a corner store doorway; the awning of a neighborhood grocer; a bookstore's painted window; the bakery's shelves; an empty schoolyard.

It is an uneasy, but necessary, routine.

After an hour, however, the incursions become more frequent, which has never happened before. I glance about from under my hood to identify our surroundings and my breath catches.

In the precious spare light I've released from the minions, I realize we're deep inside one of the first sectors to go dark, Ascension Plaza; one of the hardest hit locales in the world from what I'd heard before all communications went down. *What are we doing here?* We've never tracked through here before. Why come here now?

Before I even finish the thought, the blade flashes bright red in warning as the shadows begin to coalesce and gather around us. There are more than I can count. Panic briefly runs cold through my body. We've never fought this many at once. As they close in, the Lightblade and I become a blur of motion cutting into the enemy. I try to ignore the frantic rapid-fire thoughts on how outnumbered we are and just focus on getting from one shadow minion to the next. I remind myself to trust the blade to get me through this.

Except there seems to be no end to the shadow minions. I'm used to running as we fight, never staying in one place for very long since they've always been individualistic and sparse. When did they start working in packs? And why *here* of all places?

There just doesn't seem to be a point anymore.

Doubt begins to creep in at the edges of my consciousness.

Nothing I did made a difference.

Every swing becomes increasingly difficult. My arms feel rubbery and nerveless, and my fingers go completely numb. I feel the Lightblade begin to slip from my grasp as my vision goes hazy and swimmy like I'm looking at everything through a glass block wrapped in gauze.

Suddenly, everything goes still and quiet. I stop midstride and realize I actually can't see *anything* anymore— not because of the dark or my fatigue, but because I'm surrounded by an envelope of light. I blink rapidly, unaccustomed to the brightness, and barely make out a vaguely human figure next to me. Then, another. And another. As I regain my vision, I realize all of them are holding weapons in varying configurations and colors with one similarity: a radiant blade of pure light.

"It's okay," the figure next to me says in a calm, steady voice. "We've got your back."

The other blade wielders suddenly dart away, flinging themselves into the amassing shadow minions. After a few moments, my luminous cocoon swirls into the air like a luminous mist and sets me back onto the ground. I tentatively flex my free hand. Nothing hurts anymore and my senses are as sharp as ever. The Lightblade is excitedly thrumming at such a frequency that it almost sounds like music. We quickly join the others, though I'm hard-pressed to find available foes. These people— whoever they are— are *really* good at this.

I manage to get at two or three more minions before the fighting is over. Though we can faintly hear the opposition regrouping all around us, we take the chance to catch our breath. I'm still reeling from the fact that there is a *we* to begin with. Until now, I thought I was the only one: to find a Light weapon, to go on patrols, to fight back against the oppressive Darkness that's occupying our world.

I thought I was alone.

"It's a little hard to believe, isn't it?" asks the same calm and steady voice as if I'd spoken aloud. They chuckle softly to themselves, almost wistfully. "I couldn't believe it either. Not at first. When I first heard the rumors that someone was fighting back, I figured it was just another way for The Darkness to root out any resistance or people clinging to hope. Then, I found the Artifact— or, rather, I should say it found me."

They hold up what looks like a glowing fencing foil, slender and flexible, adapted for speed, agility, and lethal precision. At first glance, it would be easy to underestimate the weapon and its wielder, who is similarly slight and wiry. But that would be the enemy's final mistake. All I can do is nod appreciatively in silence.

"I wish I could say I was brave enough and smart enough to know what to do right then like it is in the books and movies," they continued. "Not me. I thought I was done for, that I'd be dead if I was found holding this thing. So, I did what any person scared and paranoid out of their mind did: I hid it." There was a long pause, the regret palpable in their voice and stance. "Of course, the Artifact didn't give me much of a choice in the matter, especially once the shadows attacked my neighborhood. The rest is history. Eventually, it led me to Rock over there. that's when I found out I wasn't alone in all this."

Following their finger, I see a rather large figure with broad shoulders and a sturdy bearing lounging casually against a crumbling foundation. Their weapon isn't so much a blade as a solid chunk of light stuck onto the top of a thick metal rod. I have a hard time figuring out whether the moniker, while fitting, was an homage to the person or the item they carried. They catch my gaze and raise a well-muscled arm in greeting. I wave back slowly, distracted by another spectacle I've only just noticed now that I've looked up.

We are surrounded by dozens, if not hundreds, of other people— far more than I'd initially thought.

Though everyone is hooded, each person is easily distinguishable. They are of varying shapes and sizes, garbed in an assortment of styles, and even move in specific ways. And then there are the weapons, all as distinct and singular as their wielders. The sight is breathtaking.

"Where...?" I ask haltingly, the words crashing around like I was trying to chew through a mouthful of gravel. It had been so long since I last spoke out loud. "Where did you all come from?"

"Most of us are natives of San Pacifica— different districts, though. There was an influx of folks from other megalopolises and regions over the last week or so, though. All of their stories are the same: They were all brought here by their Artifacts." They pause, tilting their head thoughtfully toward me. "I'm Needle, by the way. You got a name?"

"I... I'm..." But my voice gives out. The last person to use my name was my mother. It was also the last time I heard it spoken out loud. I hadn't needed a name since. I had almost forgotten it, along with the other parts of me that didn't involve fighting shadow minions and basic survival. Long dormant sections of my brain and memory sluggishly get back into motion. Needle waits expectantly, patiently. Finally, the neurons and synapses get all the commands in order. I speak slowly and carefully, trying my best to form the word as I remember hearing it in my mother's voice.

"Ash. My name is Ash."

I can't see it, but the smile is evident in their steady voice. "Good to meet you, Ash."

A shout of warning from the perimeter puts us back on guard. Everyone goes quiet as conversations come to an abrupt halt. Off in the distance, the shadows are amassing. They're waiting, gathering strength and numbers. There's a shift in everyone's posture as they subtly poise themselves for battle, also waiting.

In the grim silence, I can hear what sounds like… *singing*. A tingling, reverberating sensation runs up my arm and through my body. I look down at the Lightblade in my hands to find it pulsing and thrumming in time to the melody. Tentatively, I hold it up over my head like an old radio antenna. Needle, off to the side, holds up their Artifact; then Rock does the same with theirs. One by one, everyone raises their weapons. The music builds and swells with the addition of each voice until it becomes deafening.

Without warning, the shadow minions rush in as if enraged by the song. We move as one like a trained army, guided by our weapons and sheer instinct. No one's flank is unguarded; every person has backup and aid. Time seems to stand still and lose meaning in the midst of the melee. The only thing that stands out is brief, occasional glimpses of once-beautiful Ascension Plaza, now bathed in light released from vanquished shades. As long as they keep coming, we keep fighting. Fatigue has no hold on me anymore, especially now that I have others at my side.

Now, I have hope.

Just as the flood of minions seems to ebb, a terrible, grating screech brings the battle to a standstill. The shadow minions evaporate into mist, rising far above our heads. We follow them as far as our eyes allow us toward the ruined crystalline spire that was once the focal point of Ascension Plaza. It was a marvel, a work of art made from stone, steel, and glass that seamlessly blended the architectural styles of the world's cultures and religions. Now, near the shattered apex, the shades were coming together into a huge, shapeless shadow.

An eerie hush settles in. The tiny hairs on my arms and at the back of my neck stand on end. My skin prickles uneasily. Dread suddenly hangs over my every thought. Everyone around me looks about, uncertain and unsure. This wasn't just a more powerful shadow minion. It was The Darkness itself.

The Lightblade suddenly shakes violently in my hand like a tuning fork struck too hard. Its song defiantly pierces the silence. Music surges back into the void as a triumphant crescendo, filling us with a warm, effervescent energy. My grip on the Lightblade's hilt has a new resolve and strength to it. I feel like there's nothing that can stop us now. Not only that, I realize the primary source of light isn't our weapons; it's emanating from *us*.

Howling with rage, the massive shade brings one of its writhing appendages down toward us only to be thwarted by the light and the music. As one, my fellow fighters and I raise our weapons again— this time aimed at the shadow looming over us. A beam of pure light flies into the remnants of the spire, illuminating it from the inside with an ethereal glow. Magnified by the shards of fractured glass, the light grows exponentially until it erupts from the top and barrels directly into The Darkness.

It staggers back with a scream; that same terrible, grating screech echoing off the crumbling buildings around us. Chunks of shadow slough away and evaporate into the air. Victory seems impossibly near. With a bellowing roar, The Darkness slams itself down over us. We're plunged into an otherworldly dimension of complete and utter nothingness.

"WHO ARE YOU TO DEFY ME?!"

The voice leaches warmth from the very core of my being. In an instant, what precious little light we have left is extinguished. I feel the Lightblade become still and silent in my hands. It's cold to the touch; much lighter, too, like a toy you'd get as a carnival prize. Doubt and despair start to invade my thoughts again. This time, they're more insistent and pervasive; threatening to steal away and tear down the very substance of who I am.

Then again... Who am I, anyway? Some hapless schmo who happened to find a shiny thing and finds out— completely by accident— that it can slice and dice shadow minions. A nobody who, before all that, was hiding out in the rubble like a scared rat. A moron who lost everything and realized what *really* mattered far too late.

Had I learned my lesson? Was I merely playing at being the hero like a foolish child? What was *actually* at stake here? My pride? Vanity? Why *did* I take up the Lightblade and start running?

Everyone else seems to be discerning an answer to the same questions. Some are studying the dust at their feet; others are gazing up at The Darkness, lost in thought. Perhaps, there is no single, easy answer. Whatever our initial motivations were— vengeance, ego, something to do— we were all brought here for one purpose: to bring down The Darkness. It mattered that we decided to do something about our situation. And now that I think about it, I believe most, if not all, of us would have eventually acted even if we hadn't found a Light Artifact.

Earlier, I'd marveled at the myriad of people who also possessed a form of this wondrous weapon and noted how each Light Artifact seemed tailored to the wielder. I had figured it was just a feature, some sort of unknown technology that was borderline magic. After all, I'm willing to bet these folks are just like me— untested and untrained. But now it occurs to me that I may have had it backwards. It's the wielder who makes the weapon, not the other way around.

Pieces start to click into place. The Lightblade didn't come into my possession by sheer happenstance or dumb luck. It chose me, just as the other Artifacts chose the rest of us, because of something innate and intangible. My mother would not have wanted me to succumb and give in. This is not what she gave her life for. Because, this isn't how she raised me. This is *not* what she taught me.

Who are you to defy me?

This time, I have an answer. Raising my head, I scream out against the silence. "I am Ash; and I fight for my mother."

Seconds turn into minutes as the void swallows up the sound of my voice. No echo. No feedback. Nothing else happens. The Darkness is ambivalent to my statement. It judges me as below its notice and insignificant. I lower my head again, chastised and cowed. A flicker, tiny and fleeting, catches my eye. Blinking, I look again. I'm almost afraid to believe my eyes. No, it's truly there. It's real. And it's coming from *me*— not the Lightblade, not the spire or any of the crumbling buildings; but me, emerging from the center of my torso like a luminous ghost.

Others turn to look; it's difficult not to notice the growing shard of light in the inky fog. Then, they realize they have one, too. My fragment leaps down my arm, then into the Lightblade. It grows warm in my grasp again as the weapon reignites. One by one, the Artifacts blaze back to life around me; and, one by one, each wielder holds their item aloft, making an impassioned proclamation against The Darkness.

"I am River; and I fight for my family."

"I am Hammer; and I fight for my brothers and sisters."

"I am Rock; and I fight for my home."

"I am Needle; and I fight for us all."

The Darkness can no longer ignore us. It starts closing in around us, threatening to crush us into nothingness as if we were nothing more than a nuisance. The atmosphere feels close, hot, and uncomfortable. Shutting my eyes, I thrust the Lightblade above my head and hope for the best. I don't have the faintest clue of what I'm trying to accomplish; which is fine, because this is situation normal for me. The Lightblade vibrates violently in my hands again, then shatters with the effort.

A sudden, piercing cry rents the stifling air asunder. I peek out from under my eyelids in time to see a giant, glowing bird with wings of pure light and flame take shape over us. It takes off with another angry shriek, bursting clean through The Darkness. In the hole that the light left behind, seemingly far away and out of reach, we glimpse the impossible: blue sky. Tendrils of fire quickly shoot out to grab at the edges of the shadow. The more it resists, the more it loses integrity under the relentless onslaught of the light. Sunshine pours in through the holes until we're surrounded by warmth and energy, blinking and squinting and shouting with glee.

All around us, pieces of The Darkness dissolve and sublimate. Glittering bits of light emancipated from its shroud dance about before rocketing off into the distance. We don't know what's going to happen tomorrow, or what the next step is. What we *do* know is that we have today, and we have each other.

It's all we could ever want– and all we could ever hope for.

Monday Motivation #108 by Kévin Jean-Philippe

WHAT WE'RE MEANT FOR

Journey afar
Return to
The stars

Give not
Into worriment
Remember
Who you are

You were made
For more
Than this

Created
By God
To know laughter

To know bliss

-Adrienne T. Nugent

Angel's Wings

Hopeful flight
On wings of strength
Soaring heights
All fears erased
Your subtle dreams
Your heart's desire
Flying high
Into the sky
Oh, happy day
Oh, grateful heart
There's no dismay
Your fears depart

-K.N. Nguyen

MAGIC

Saviors' souls, tarot cards

Candles burning, my guitar

Strings are strumming, incense burning

Spirits speaking, spirits learning

Magic moon, God is calling

Midnight magic, rainbow fragments

The dusk is not changing, it is stalling

Into a new Earth, Angels falling

-Deanna Stinson

HEALER

By Mel Tong

I studied to be a healer before I knew of my powers. When I was fifteen, a great horn grew on my forehead. Thankfully, humans have no power to see it. It's been years, and I still find it gross. Unicorns as plushies are great, but in reality, I can't even sleep on my belly anymore; let alone wear hats. It gives me headaches.

I interned at a hospital in my small town. Every day, I come home, exhausted, no one wiser that I used my healing powers with a subtle touch while taking doing something routine like taking their blood pressure. But even we unicorns have limits. I can only treat issues that would normally heal over time. Unfortunately, cancer was not one of them.

I phoned my friend, Miya Lee Cyrus. She already lived many lifetimes by the time I was born. Recently, she was reborn again. I've always been interested in phoenixes. I imagine lives must be so lonely, so when I met Miya, I was excited to begin a friendship that would span centuries.

I knew she would be able to help me. You see, Grandma Victoria had cancer. I felt it when we held hands.

"Oh, botherbug. I'm all right," she said as she pat my hand gently. Just the other day she was patching a worn roof. Grandma may have been old, but she was so spry.

I didn't want to tell her the news. That she had cancer. Miya owed me, a boon from her past life. I knew we needed to act before Grandma got any worse.

"Are you crazy, Alice?" Miya asked, her dark curls bounced as she shook her head incredulously.

"Crazy serious, Miya."

"I've never done this before," Miya said. "It's very dangerous."

"We have to try. At this point, all we have left is hope. What do we have to lose?" My words poured forth in a wave of emotion. Grandma's condition came on so suddenly. I knew I would do anything to help her get better.

Miya watched me, her eyes locking onto mine. "All right. I'm in," Miya said, shaking my hand. "I'd shame my people anyway if I didn't live up to the old saying: Hope dies when the final ember is out. My flame still burns strong."

Later that day, we spiked Grandma's tea with a sedative to help her sleep. I felt so guilty, so I gave her some of my famous cookies, fresh from the oven. The warm biscuit generously coated in caramel, drizzled with dark chocolate and a generous sprinkle of crushed coconut were Grandma's favorite. I even put a few aside for Miya as a thank you for her help.

I massaged Grandma's lump after she'd laid down for her nap. Oh, how my fingers wanted to work their magic on her, but I made sure that I didn't wake her from her nap prematurely. If I reversed the effects of the sedative, she'd probably feel everything. Grabbing a marker, I drew a circle on her neck.

"Here."

Miya nodded and gently touched Grandma's neck. As her slender finger touched the flesh, beads of sweat formed on Grandma's brow. I watched Miya's eyes narrow in concentration as she worked to keep Grandma's flesh from burning.

Grandma's eyes fluttered open, her hand going to her neck.

"Are you okay, Grandma?" I spoke calmly as my fingers touched her neck. As Grandma rested on her palms, I worked quickly to soothe the pain from Miya's work, while treating the affected spot.

Grandma lowered herself back onto her bed, a serene smile on her face. "No, nothing is wrong, botherbug," she mumbled. Closing her eyes, Grandma fell into a deep sleep with the help of the sedative.

Smiling to Miya, we quietly left the room. All was well. All I needed was faith.

Untitled

- 33 -

By Emma Cepeda

WHITE LILY

A cloud becomes a white lily in the sky

A fragile moment colored like selenite

Time passes before my eyes into

The daydream moonlight

-Deanna Stinson

I BECAME

Darkness all around me falling
Lifetime spent on belly, crawling
Instincts said to make it end
Trapped here now in my own head
Before may not have been so bad
Compared to this hot, stifling mad
What have I done?
Where have I gone?
Bright days grown black
And I can't get back.

But wait…
What's this?

Just as my whole world was ending
Felt a strength all through my being
Scraping, chewing, sloughing through
The darkness I'd nearly succumbed to
Sun in sky, breeze in air
Breathing deep, I begin to care
Unfurling gossamer wings – that's new!
Flowers call me with morning dew
Right when I thought that I would die
Instead, I became a butterfly.

-T. M. Lowe

A PLACE FOR A LONELY GIRL

By Adrienne T. Nugent

Daylia Charmwright, a girl with a peculiarly spelled name, lived alone in a peculiarly odd house in a peculiar town filled with peculiar people, all of whom didn't seem particularly very nice.

Now, it just so happens that the townsfolk's case of unkindness was due to the fact that they didn't quite appreciate "abnormalities" or "oddities" in polite conversation. When speaking of odd traits, one could say Daylia had many; not that this mattered much to her. Nor does it to me, which is why I see no need to mention them.

Now, what did bother her was the fact that she lived alone. In a place that was a house, but not a home. As luck would have it, a day came where Daylia spied a peculiar tuft of trees not too far from the peculiar town while walking her pet rock. Remember those traits I told you didn't matter? Well, walking her invisible pet rock is one of them. Back to the story at hand, she decided to take a chance, as children are oft to do, and walk into the peculiar woods. There, staring back at her, were all manners of creatures, all of whom looked quite happy to see her.

There were all sorts: there were nymphs, sprites, animal spirits, even woodlings! If you don't know what any of these are, I apologize; I am not here to give lessons on mystical beings, I am here to tell a story. So, you will just have to do without, I'm afraid. Now, back to the story at hand.

Daylia had a new sense of purpose, as she would spend her days visiting the forest, playing amongst the trees and with the sprites who lived there. Little did she realize that the more time she spent there, the more she changed.

When I say "changed", I'm not referring to a character trait as much as an actual physical change. It so happened that her love for the creatures was rubbing off on her, so to speak. She found that as the days passed, she was no longer fully human. Her ears turned fox-like, her fingernails were more like little claws now, and she had grown a tail!

Now, the peculiar town is not known for liking things that are, well… peculiar. When they saw Daylia's new "features", they saw it as an opportunity to run her out of town. So, in the middle of the night, when the moon was full, the townsfolk knocked forcefully on the young girl's house.

Daylia, being the smart girl that she is, had already suspected this would happen and took it upon herself to pack her important things and leave the town that never felt like home. Into the woods she went and, lo, there were her friends waiting for her with open arms. Interestingly, the townsfolk could never figure out where Daylia had gone off to nor did they truly care. Hmm, it's almost as if the forest couldn't be seen by those who have rotten hearts.

Daylia Charmwright, a girl with a peculiarly spelled name, lived with her friends in a uniquely interesting house in a lovely forest, filled with magic, all of which was very nice and most importantly…

Felt like home.

Monday Motivation #96 by Kévin Jean-Philippe

PHARAOH

Scarab drawing the truth in the sand

Wings over time in a dream land

I rush to the Pharaoh

The hourglass in my hand

I sink slowly in quicksand

Like white dust of a borderland

Kings scatter into my eyes

I fall into prayers

Of another time

-Deanna Stinson

TIME LIKE A STREAM

Time
Like an
Ever rolling
Stream

Bears all
My worries away

They fly
Forgotten
As if
They were
Petals
In the wind

Ever moving
In the changing
Of the seasons

Through flowery fields
Kissed by morning's light

Shining facets of life

Hope carried wingless
Brightening the nights

Forever changed
Into new purpose
As they fade away
Into memory

Time
Like a
Stream

Soothes

Heals

-Adrienne T. Nugent

ONCE MORE 'ROUND ETERNITY

By Anthony Amundson

ROUND 1

Eternity. If I close my eyes I can picture its surface, or at least what is left of it. The scars and craters of untold years of mining have left the rock a desiccated husk. Perhaps the name had some meaning to whoever did the naming, but for all of us doomed to forever accompany Eternity there is an undeniable irony. We squabble and fight here in this forgotten chunk of metal, while it orbits round Eternity, never ever to stop.

Old Red used to say we are like some place called Georgia. I've never heard anyone else use that name, but I'll believe him. I figure every generation must have somewhere to put those who don't belong, the unwelcome, the criminal. I asked him what happened to this Georgia and he said it became part of a great nation. I'll take a little more convincing before I believe that one.

Besides, everyone always said not to believe everything you hear from Old Red. "Not quite sane", people'd say: "he's stared down at the surface of Eternity for too long" or "ten thousand rounds leaves its mark." 'Course I should be thankful. What sane man would have taken me in, given me a home, much less taught me to write. Without him, there's no way you'd be reading this, whoever you might be.

Even if no one reads this, I'm still going to write it, one round each day before I go to bed. Red was always encouraging me to write, so I suppose it's a fitting way to honor the old man's memory. Besides, what else am I going to do, locked away in this prison within a prison. I guess I should be grateful Elia left me a terminal so I can at least type these words.

ROUND 2

I figure I better introduce myself. My name is Loben Bos. Bos isn't a real name, it's a label: "Born on Ship." When the crew isn't sure of your parents, the name Bos is the best they can do. It's not like they ever cared all that much how many children are born. When a prisoner is on a work detail in the ship proper, you better bet the crew will be watching. You put that same prisoner down here in the hold and the crew could care less. There's a couple thousand of us down here. Sometimes children live their entire lives down here in the slums without the crew even knowing they exist. Unfortunately, the crew noticed me. I'm not sure what stood out. I'm pretty typical for a Bos child, dark hair, kinda scrawny, covered in dust and grime. Whatever it was, I got selected.

Ever since the loss of Earth, back before I was born, we have been on our own up here. The Warden managed to keep the place running, but sometimes he had to replace members of the crew. With only those of us down in the hold to choose from, he preferred recruiting from the Bos. I'm still a little young to be formally drafted into the crew, but I am close enough that he had his eye on me. I got choice assignments for work detail, better food than most, that sort of thing. It sounds great, but didn't do me any favors when it comes to surviving down here. These last few years I've stayed pretty close to the hold's entrance. The farther into the slums you go, the worse it gets. If I go too far back, I might disappear.

ROUND 3

It's been three rounds since Xander took over the ship. Three rounds since he declared himself Warden. Three rounds since he took his revenge on those who had oppressed him, killing the crew and anyone associated with them. It has also been three rounds since I was forced into this prison within a prison, in order to avoid being killed for my own ties to the crew.

I've had plenty of opportunity to be bored in my life, but the last few rounds have been something else. Standard ship chores aren't anyone's idea of exciting, but at least they are something to do. At this point I think I would be happy to clean 'cycler slime off the air processors if it meant I could get out of this room. At the same time, I know I should be happy simply to have survived the takeover.

The only reason I am still alive is Elia. She used to visit Old Red regularly as I was growing up. She would drape her small frame across some of the makeshift furniture while listening to some of Old Red's latest poetry or just shooting the breeze. From time to time she would fix something up in Red's cell. Whatever she had done in her previous life, she seemed to have a knack for fixing things.

Anyway, when everything fell apart a few rounds ago, she appeared out of nowhere right next to me. As the first shouts of the fledgling riot sounded, she was already leading me through the twisting passages of the slums. The paths were nearly empty as she led me deeper into the slums. We passed through sections I had never dared to visit, and then further. When we at last stopped, the corridor walls were hardly visible through graffiti, garbage, and other ruins from decades of neglect. Only a few of the lights overhead still worked.

Stepping into Elia's cell had been like stepping into another world. Inside the door it was immaculate. The lights worked, the floor was clean, and all of the original paneling was still in place. There was even an actual sleeping pallet like I had seen in the crew barracks, and while the bedding looked threadbare, it was still carefully made up.

Elia must have noticed my shock. "This has been my cell since I was first sent up here. I wasn't much older than you then."

She approached a wall. With a move too subtle for me to see, she managed to pop a section of wall paneling loose. She must have had some sort of tool in her hand. Those panels normally didn't budge at all, even if hit by the weight of a thrown man. I had seen such firsthand more than once.

She gestured for me to go through the opening and, after a moment's hesitation, I did. The room beyond was a miniature garden. Plants grew in pots, boxes, anything that could hold some dirt. At the center of the room was a gigantic thick-stemmed plant (which I have since found out is called a tree). It is unlike anything I have ever seen in any of the ship's greenhouses.

"I'll check back in later tonight," Elia continued. "There's food in the cabinet. Don't eat it all, and don't touch the plants." With that the panel was back in place and she was gone. I put out a hand and pushed on the panel. It didn't move.

ROUND 4

I finally got some relief from the boredom today. Elia spent a few extra minutes with me and showed me how to care for her plants. I had strictly followed her order to not touch the plants (although I had already spent plenty of time looking at them). Perhaps she has taken pity on me and wants to give me something to do. Whatever the reason for the change of heart, I am grateful and will be very careful to follow her instructions exactly. I already owe her so much for hiding me here. The last thing I would want to do would be to harm something she values so highly.

ROUND 5

More worrying news from Elia today.

It has been only a few rounds since the old Warden was assassinated and Xander's fledgling dictatorship is already developing a serious competitor. Given my own situation, I should have been happy to hear this. Unfortunately, the competitor is the only faction I can think of who would be worse.

The Doomsayers have always been a shadow on ship society. They say that the death of Earth was fated, that the survival of this little chunk of humanity was an accident. Some of the more crazy even suggest this is an accident which should be fixed. Under the Warden they were always an elusive rumor. No one would admit to being in their ranks. People who did had a tendency to disappear. Usually with no comment from the ship's crew.

With the Warden gone, it sounds like they have decided to come out into the open and there are a lot more of them than anyone thought. It doesn't sound like they quite have the numbers to compete with Xander directly. But, with the Doomsayers, control of the ship might not be their objective. Their goals are sure to be more destructive in nature. As I go to sleep, I actually find myself wishing Xander luck. Hopefully he can get them under control. Maybe he will even be weakened in the process.

One can always hope.

ROUND 6

It was a slow round. Elia had nothing to report from outside my cell. Surprisingly, I might have something to report from inside.

As part of my general duties, I've been 'caring for' plants in the ship's gardens as far back as I can remember. Somehow, though, caring for Elia's plants is different. I measure out the fertilizer to the last drop. I am careful not to spill when adding water. Elia has entrusted me with this little bit of her life, and I can see how much she cares for it. It is almost as if, by entrusting them to me, Elia has made them 'my' plants.

Is this what Elia created the garden for? Is this why Red was always writing his poetry? Does everyone need some small thing to focus on, to call their own as they go about life's more mundane tasks? This isn't a bad thought to go to sleep with. Not bad at all.

ROUND 7

Something is happening. Elia has been gone most of the day, and there is a lot more noise out in the hall then normal. When I place my ear against the hull of the ship I can hear the occasional rumble. The sound is muted and far away, but it doesn't sound like anything I have heard on the ship before. I can't seem to stop wondering what is happening. Even writing doesn't seem to steady my mind tonight. I just can't stop wondering: What is going on? Does it have to do with the Doomsayers? What will I do if it does?

So far there are no answers...

Round 7 (part 2)

I had finally managed to drowse for some time, but woke to find myself thrown from the blankets that served as my bed. I tumbled across the floor, stopping painfully when I ran into the opposite wall of the room. I rose immediately in a crouch, adrenaline coursing and ready to confront my attacker. Yet the room was empty. It was only at this point I perceived the fading echoes of enumerable pops and bangs coming from the ship all around me. I was having a hard time keeping my balance, too. It was like something was pushing me toward one side of the room.

The realization hit me. Something had happened to the ship. No one had pushed me out of my bed. Instead something had pushed the entire ship. Even as I thought this, I was already going through the normal disaster checklist, which was drilled into us as children until it was as natural as breathing. Fortunately, I found nothing immediately wrong. Gravity still worked, there was no hiss of leaking atmosphere, no roar of fire, and no harm to myself other than a nasty bruise on my elbow. I almost risked shouting a question to Elia. Surely, she would have returned by now, but would anyone else hear me?

Before I could decide whether to call out, the panel popped open. It was Elia. Thankfully she was unhurt, and after I confirmed I was also fine, we turned our attention to righting a few of the plants which had been toppled by the shock. For its part the tree had grown into various girders and pipes of the roof long ago and seemed unfazed by whatever had happened.

We both guessed at what could have shaken the ship so strongly, but neither of us could really do more than guess. I had no information at all, and as it turned out Elia didn't have much more. She knew Xander had moved against the Doomsayers, and that there had been running fights throughout the ship. Because of this, she had spent much of the day hiding in another part of the slums.

With so little real content to go on, the conversation eventually steered away from the ship entirely. Elia ended up talking about herself, and I ended up mostly listening. Not once in the time I have known her was she ever this talkative. I even got a few vague hints she and Red had known each other back on Earth. For my part, I was plenty happy to listen. Anything to help take my mind away from worrying.

Eventually Elia excused herself and returned to her side of the panel to sleep. I've been getting more and more tired as I write this entry as well.

Good night.

ROUND 8

I'm going to have to break with tradition and write a morning entry. We are all still here, but I can hear that the commotion outside continues. Up till now Elia had seemed content to hide in her cell. I hadn't heard her leave, and neither had she popped in to talk to me. This changed just a few moments ago.

Someone paid Elia a visit. With the panel in place I couldn't quite hear well enough to know what was said. I could hear when the conversation was suddenly cut off by Elia's cell door closing. I haven't heard anything since. Whoever the visitor was and whatever they wanted, Elia must have gone with them. I can't help but envision what could be happening out in the rest of the ship or what trouble could befall Elia out there. I know she has lived here longer than I have been alive, but I still find myself surprisingly unable to focus on anything else.

ROUND 8 (PART 2)

Elia returned. I am not sure she even stopped in her cell before coming straight into the refuge. She was in such a hurry to share her news that she didn't even bother to put the panel back in place. In fact, she is still in the refuge with me now, although she is busying herself with caring for her plants. I think this more of a way for her to calm down than anything else. The plants have received more than enough care from both of us in the last few days. Then again, I can't blame her for wanting something calming to do. Honestly my writing is providing the same purpose to me. After what she just found out we could all use a little calming.

The Doomsayers made their move last night. They fought their way out of the hold and into the rest of the ship. By all accounts they were soundly defeated by Xander's men, but not before they all managed to gather together in one of the garden holds. Somehow, they created a bomb. It was strong enough to breach even the hardened hull of the ship, and the entire bay depressurized, taking all of them and a good chunk of the garden with it. It sounds like all the Doomsayers were in that one push. If there are any left aboard, they aren't being obvious (not that I would blame them for hiding at this point).

Shockingly, the loss of a garden wasn't the biggest news. What came after had forced Elia to go see for herself. Eternity was not where it was supposed to be. During each orbit Eternity gets bigger and smaller with clockwork precision. In fact, these rounds are actually used as a clock by most of us, with the point when Eternity is largest defined as midday.

My body tells me it is near midday now. Elia agrees with this, but when she finally found Eternity in the sea of stars, it was both a size and position to suggest it was still near midnight. There is only one possible explanation. The shock that hit the ship last night was caused by the Doomsayer's bomb letting a vast amount of air escape from the ship all at once. Like an old-fashioned rocket, this had pushed on the ship, changing its orbit.

If Eternity still looked small the change must have been significant. What no one seemed to know was how significant. Was the ship now free of Eternity, destined to coast through space in high earth orbit forever? Was the new orbit simply different but stable? Or in the worst case, was the new orbit unstable, meaning the ship would shortly crash? Surely some of the crew could have figured out the answer to these questions in minutes. I, for one, have no way to know one way or another. I suppose I will just have to wait and find out the old-fashioned way.

ROUND 9

I am not sure why I am bothering to write this. The logical part of my brain tells me it is meaningless. Why write something no one is ever going to have the chance to read? The logical part of my brain knows this for a fact yet the human side of my brain insists on doing something. The logical side of my brain acknowledges that writing will keep me occupied but the human side sees more to it than that. I feel driven to complete the writing. Now that I have started to tell the tale I worry I will let you all down if I don't finish. So, for you, audience, I write the events of the last few hours, even knowing there is no way you will ever be able to read them.

> Not long after I put down the terminal from writing the last entry, one of Xander's patrols arrived. They were probably just making a show of force around the ship, trying to reinforce the strength of Xander's image after the events of last night. When they burst through the door, we all looked at each other for a bit. They seemed stunned, whether it was the hidden chamber or simply the neatness of the room given the corridor outside, I do not know. Perhaps they would have simply taken it all in stride, said their piece and then left, but then one of them recognized me.
>
> The stunner was out of the guard's holster in a moment, and the other guard echoed his companion's action after only a moment more. A few quick words passed between them. Then the guard who had drawn first ran from the room. The other continued to cover us with his stunner. He was no dummy, and didn't let us even approach the missing panel separating the refuge from the cell proper.

In what seemed like no time at all, the door to the cell opened again, admitting Xander himself. He had never looked what anyone would call nice, but now his face was truly fearsome. Veins bulged, and a flush of red colored his cheeks and spread to his temples. At the same time his eyes had a sunken look that betrayed deepest exhaustion. Stimhead, some part of my brain noted. Stims could keep you awake and focused, but they also made you more volatile. Xander had been plenty volatile to start with.

I figured we were dead where we stood. It is very possible Xander expected this too. At a flick of his finger the guards had us in their grasp, unable to move. Then he stepped through the open panel, entering the refuge proper. Elia writhed against her captors. I remained pliant, but could only imagine how she felt. I felt like my world was ending, but this wasn't truly my refuge that was being invaded.

Xander carried a large steel rod, which he now hefted. Purportedly it was the rod he had killed the Warden with. The rod went up, but was preempted by a shout from out in the hall. If anything, Xander's face got even darker, but he remained as he was, rod poised overhead. Without turning he bellowed, demanding to know what the interruption was about.

Then came the words. Those words that doomed us all. Eternity was getting bigger again, getting bigger fast. Even without the crew it was now certain, the ship would crash.

With a shout, Xander brought the rod down, not on me or Elia, but on the tree. Its wood was strong, but Xander swung a mighty blow. Wood yielded before steel, shattering into innumerable pieces. A feral shriek rose from Elia as the rod came up again, but even her cry was then lost beneath the harsh tang of a stunner discharge. I felt a tingle on any exposed skin, but that was all: I hadn't been the target.

The noise sounded again, and then a third time. Before me Xander was sinking to his knees, eyes wide, mouth open as if to ask a question. Then his eyes closed and he started to fall forward, the bar falling from his nerveless fingers. Behind him, two guards were also falling to the ground. A third was just turning back toward us, his stunner still glowing white after multiple uses. "Peace Eternal!" He shouted, the rallying cry of the Doomsayers.

The guards holding Elia and I didn't have stunners. They had set them aside before approaching us. Both must have come to the same conclusion, and launched into simultaneous dives toward the doomsayer. The Doomsayer got off one more shot, knocking out the guard on Elia's side. Elia got caught in some of the backwash shouting as she started to sink to the ground. Then both guards and the doomsayer crashed together, collapsing in a tangle.

Now was our chance. Everyone else was either down or fighting for their lives. I wasted no time gathering up Elia and making a break for the door. I wasn't quite big enough and she wasn't quite small enough where I could carry her. Thankfully she was still half conscious. She could carry just enough of her own weight where I could guide us both down hall after hall.

The sounds of the fighting faded behind us, and then once more I heard the tang of a stunner. Who had won, I didn't know. At this point I hoped they had all been stunned so it would give us time to get farther away. Elia mumbled something to herself at the noise, but I couldn't make out the words.

We kept moving. I didn't know the halls, and turned at random at every junction. I feared at any moment we would be confronted by a guard or even another of the slum's denizens. Yet no one met us. Perhaps the recent sounds of stunners being fired had scared everyone off. Perhaps we were just lucky.

Either way, when I turned a corner and was confronted by an airlock I breathed a sigh of relief. On the other side was space, but in the airlock itself was safety. There was no way to open an airlock during cycle except from inside the lock itself. It was fail-safe.

I walked us into the airlock, smashing the cycle button then worked on getting Elia settled in. I did this, Elia's continued mumblings suddenly rose back to a shriek, all trace of the stunner's affects fading away. She pushed me away, then launched herself through the slowly closing airlock door. Shocked and caught off balance, I tumbled to the floor. By the time I righted myself she was gone.

"Elia!" I shouted, just before the final boom announced the door as sealed. Picking myself up off the ground I ran to the door. Peering through the small window, I saw nothing but the ruined corridors of the slums. Elia had vanished, leaving me alone in this airlock. I wasn't even sure I could find my way back to her rooms. I hadn't really had spare focus for memorizing our path as I ran.

Why had she fled? To where? What was I supposed to do? I felt suddenly weak. Withdrawing from the window, I settled against the wall of the airlock, face in my hands. Between fingers I saw the airlock status readout, patiently blinking 'ready to depressurize'. Otherwise, all was unexpected calm. I closed my eyes.

No pursuit arrived. Outside my refuge, the ship occasionally shook or trembled as her occupants spent their final hours obliterating each other. What if they had already succeeded, I wondered. What if even now I was the last person left alive on the ship? Or, the last person left alive, period?

Loneliness filled me, and I cried.

I don't know how much time passed. It might have been minutes, it might have been an hour or more. Yet with time the tears stopped. I was still here. I could still act. What my acts would accomplish I did not know, but I could not abide staying where I was forever. For all I knew, Elia was still out there somewhere. Didn't I owe it to her to at least try to find her?

I opened my eyes. Through clearing tears, my sight fell on the small window set into the exterior door of the airlock. There was light showing through it. Rising, I walked un-steadily toward it. The light was Eternity, shining more brightly than ever because it was closer than ever. I knew what I had to do, and I knew I didn't have much time left to do it. Turning my back on the window, I canceled the airlock cycle. The inner door opened and I strode through.

I made my way as best I could. In places the corridors were near impassible with debris. In a couple places the blockages were almost certainly intentional, built in a mad rush to defend against now vanished threats. In a few places the losers of these short battles joined the rest of the general clutter. Of the living, there was no trace. I did my best to avoid focusing on anything too closely and pressed on.

As I moved, I discovered I could remember my path most of the time, only having to double back after wrong turns a couple of times. I would never have been able to keep up with the speed Elia could have made through these halls, and for that matter I can only assume she had ran for her quarters. If she hadn't there was no telling where she might have gone. No, she must have gone to her quarters.

I was fully confident I was only a turn or two away when I turned a corner and stopped dead, gasping aloud. Xander sat against the wall of the corridor, eyes closed, but facing right toward me. I was so shocked, so frightened that it took me a moment to notice the rod resting carelessly next to him. A red coating covered it. The same color permeated some of Xander's clothes. I remained frozen, transfixed. Xander has been such a threat for such a time. Despite what my eyes were seeing, it just couldn't be possible that he was gone.

A sound from my right brought the present back into focus. The sound came again. It sounded like someone crying, sobbing quietly. I looked, and there was Elia, crumpled into a ball and wedged into the most shadowed part of the corridor. She seemed so tiny, I was certain I wouldn't have noticed her if she hadn't made a sound. Crouching before her, I whispered her name.

Her eyes opened, and I almost fell backward. Where I had expected sorrow, I found fury. The look was so intense that when she sprung up from where she hid, I actually felt a moment of fear. The moment passed in an instant, though, as she reached me and wrapped me in a hug, nearly crushing me with an intensity I would not have thought possible.

"They beat me to him." She whispered, slowly. "They got here only moments before I did, Xander's senior henchmen. They killed the surviving guard, who had been trying to pull Xander's body down the hall. Then they killed Xander. They beat him to death while he was still unconscious. He must not have treated his friends any better than his enemies." Elia let out a short bark that might charitably have been called a laugh, then continued, the intensity returning to her voice. "But he should have been mine. He destroyed my garden, ruined my home, threatened both me and you."

Elia seemed to run out of words, quivering with frustration. For a moment we simply stayed where we were. I couldn't rightfully figure out what to think. Xander was gone, Elia was a wreck, and of course, Eternity was coming. I couldn't begin to guess how to help Elia, I couldn't even figure out how to help myself. It was all too much for anyone.

And with that realization came clarity.

"Let it go," I whispered. "We have so little time remaining, maybe not even a full hour. Don't spend it this way." I could barely believe the words myself. They had occurred to me in a moment of insight, and they sounded ridiculous to me even as I spoke them. But as much as I wanted to disbelieve them, I couldn't find fault in them.

"Only an hour?" Elia managed to ask, barely even a whisper.

I nodded. A few more moments passed.

"Then come with me. I still have something to do."

She released me and rose, stepping carefully around Xander. I followed, a little dazed, not really thinking, just acting. I didn't know what she needed to do, but I could follow and see. Wordlessly she led me to her ruined cabin, and then through it and into the garden.

The garden was just as bad as I had feared. The tree's stout but brittle wood had been truly wrecked by Xander's might. Pieces lay everywhere. A few of the other plants had even been knocked about by the flying pieces. Elia shot right through these without stopping, going for her storage shelf, then ransacking it. Containers, a purloined trowel, and scraps of paper went flying. Then she turned, a smile pushing through her tear-stained face. In her hand she held a small nut.

"Will you help me plant this?" She asked. "For the future."

I paused for a second, taken aback at the absurdity of the question. Then I felt a smile try to creep onto my face as well. What better thing was there to do? Caring for her garden was what brought Elia joy. Truly, what better thing did I have to do?

Elia poured some soil from the pot holding the ruined stump into a smaller pot, and then handed me the seed. The soil felt good under my fingers as I pushed the nut into it. Then I stepped back as Elia busied herself with cleaning and repairing her garden as best she could.

As I stepped back, I noticed the terminal Elia had given me lying discarded on the ground. To my relief it still turned on and hadn't been broken in the fight.

And now you are up to date, whoever you might be. Elia is done with her gardening. The ruined tree went in the outer room and the panel had been set in place, sealing us away from all the horror beyond. Meanwhile I have wrote what I must. Both of us are resting now, content to savor the success of our efforts. I just realized that for the first time in my life there is no governing authority over me. For the few hours since I left the air-lock, I have been free to choose my own path. I think I have made the best of the choices available to me. Against all expectation, I am content.

By Emma Cepeda

DROWNING IN A PAST LIFE

Barefoot in wet mud like clay

Green rolling hills at dusk

My soul is not going to stay

Bound into the valley of Earth

Magic is sweet and it is bitter

Falling angels' tears lead you on

Stars sparkle and burst into glitter

Shapeshifter, dreamer, waterlily bound

Lanterns gliding across a marsh

Will they reach the other side?

Or will I...

-Deanna Stinson

POWERFUL

Fearless
I know that I can do anything that
I set my mind to
Nothing
Nothing can stop me
I am a force that knows no bounds
That is tied down by nothing
I am powerful
When hope turns to despair
I may dim
But my light will never go out
I am powerful
I will push forward
Toppling obstacles
Conquering mountains
I am a force to be reckoned with
I am powerful
I am unstoppable
I am unconquerable
I will shine bright
I will be strong
I will go on

-K.N. Nguyen

ANGELS OF MERCY

By LS Fellows

"**O**n that day in May, I grew up. Fast. Had I known the fate awaiting me, I'd never have clambered aboard that pretty train. It was a journey to change my life, to shape my future and to define me as the man I would become."

Valerie paused and glanced at her audience. Had it been the right decision to read an excerpt from Cousin Eric's notes? Only time would tell. She ran her tongue over dry lips, then recommenced her reading from the loose-leaf dossier she'd inherited along with the building.

"Days before we sat at our desks, still as statues, while a lady from the government - as nine-year-olds, none of us knew what that meant - addressed the class. Wearing a grey dress beneath a matching jacket, a badge on the lapel I'd seen before but couldn't place, she spoke in a booming voice. No gestures, no warmth, no smile. We would be taking a trip to a hilltop village to take the air, she told us. Her dark hair was pulled back into a severe bun and her steely-eyed expression, as serious as an owl, meant we didn't dare ask questions. We nodded in unison when she enquired if we'd understood. I feared any other response would have earned her wrath. My schoolmates thought likewise. But as soon as she left, we begged our teacher to explain.

"Marianne, whose smile cheered us like sunshine after that grey woman's gloom, gathered us all together and promised us a great adventure. A train journey awaited us, through the leafy forests where magical creatures roamed. Our excitement bubbled like a tea kettle on the boil as we headed home, brimming with hope for a marvellous escapade in the coming days.

"The day arrived and, with it, a cloudless blue sky. Not even the world's worst storm could have dampened my enthusiasm at that point. Although Mother's tearful farewell and Father staying home from work to see me off brought frown lines to my forehead. They dismissed my puzzlement with a luncheon box assuring me my favourite treats were inside. But they weren't alone in acting oddly. The community hall overflowed with parents and grandparents waving us goodbye as we fell into line behind Marianne, whose job it was to ensure none of us strayed. My attention soon drifted when Peter, my best friend since infancy, began whistling; it was a dreadful din, destined to bring rain later.

"We reached the station far too early, jollied along by high spirits and the girls singing. What more could we have wanted? A day out of school and a grand adventure ahead. We would have waited forever.

"How I wished I'd taken more time to say goodbye. To have held Mama longer, breathed in her perfume and lain my head on her shoulder awhile. To have hugged Papa instead of shaking his hand when he ruffled my hair. I'd tried to be so mature, not realising how soon I would have to grow up."

Valerie reached for the glass of water. Despite having rehearsed this many times, the heartfelt emotions still brought a tightness to her chest and a dryness to her throat.

"The station heaved with activity; men in dark suits carrying briefcases paced up and down the platform, trying to flag down the stationmaster or his staff. Smoke billowed, puffing its way towards us, caught in the downwind, remnant of a recently departed train. Was this the reason we were heading for cleaner air? Would a day out make that much difference? Noone had clarified the reason for our journey, not Marianne, not my parents and not that miserable-looking government lady. Our entire schooling since her visit had focused on the great adventure before us, but still our questions remained unanswered, with 'wait and see' soon becoming the most irritating phrase ever."

Hushed murmurings from her new staff seemed to appreciate the boyish humour and gave her chance to catch her breath before resuming.

"An approaching train brought with it great excitement. We jumped as high as we could to catch a glimpse of it, elbows colliding and heads bashing. But we didn't care. Then came the most piercing sound, not like the trains that usually passed through our town. This one was altogether different. Its long, drawn-out whistle, so loud as to make the trees tremble and the ground shake, sent us into a frenzy of gleeful laughter. Marianne resembled an octopus, pulling us all into line again. I'd never been as excited about a trip. I never would be again.

"The stationmaster shouted over the madness and the dark-suited men stomped to the back of the platform, allowing us our first proper view of the train. Mine was not the only jaw to fall open. Smoke spewing from the front soon remedied that. We coughed and coughed, exaggerating its effect on us as only children could.

"Marianne led us onto the platform. As the smoke evaporated, the train materialised, shiny green as opposed to the regular blue and off-white ones that trawled the city's tracks. As though delivered by the fairies themselves, the promise of magical creatures ahead never seemed more plausible. Until then, we had listened to our teacher's tales with the exuberance of the nine-year-olds we were, but even we weren't so gullible as to believe them to be true. Bedecked in multicoloured tinsel and fresh, fragrant spring flowers, the open carriages might have been created by my hero, Hans Christian, himself.

"We clambered aboard, like rats up a drainpipe. Inside, wooden bench seats glistened, all shiny and slippery. Peter and I agreed we'd found the perfect setting for playing the game 'and, ... one fell off' later. Laughter filled every nook and cranny. We poked our heads out of the carriage, wrapping our arms around the metal bar so as not to fall out. Trees towered over us on one side, its topmost branches touching the sky like Mama's feather duster reaching for the high ceilings of our home. Some taller boys swung from the yellow rails above, their feet kicking at us. Until Marianne climbed aboard and instructed us to sit down.

"She'd never been strict with us before; it wasn't her nature. So, we took our seats without fuss. Her cheeks, red and puffy, glistened with dampness. Something was wrong. I knew it then. This was no regular school outing. I watched her face for a sign, but all I saw were the tears welling in her blotchy, blue eyes. 'Be still, please,' she said, 'I have something to tell you.' Her voice, quiet as it was, was drowned by the shrillness of the whistle as the train left the platform.

"More smoke wafted into our carriage. No one coughed this time. We sat in silence as the train weaved through the leafy woodland, cool shadows casting their darkness upon us. There was rain ahead. Onto the wooden mountain track we turned. The wheels clicked and clacked, but there was no noise from us. Marianne's sad and grave expression had all but tranquilised us into a state of stillness."

Valerie had to take another sip of water, the lump in her throat threatening to steal her breath completely. She raised her head and saw her onlookers divert their gaze or offer an encouraging smile, empathising with her struggle. She took a deep breath and read on.

"An adjoining door to our carriage opened. I hadn't even noticed it there; such had been my focus on the slippery benches and railings. A lady, younger than Mama but I guessed a few years older than Marianne, stepped through. Long, loose dark hair fell over her shoulders, and she smiled - a warm, inviting smile that suggested everything was going to be fine. Maybe Marianne was unwell, maybe I'd imagined the sorrow in her gestures, the stiffness in her actions. Maybe my vivid imagination had gone into overdrive. Though I doubted it.

"The lady sat beside Marianne, wrapping an arm around her quaking shoulders. 'Boys and girls, I have something for you. But, first, let me assure you that you're all safe and you're here because your parents loved you all so very, very much. Too much to let you be harmed in any way.' She read out our names, one by one, and handed out letters. When my turn came, we locked eyes. Owlish, grey circles stared back at me, but not cold as the first time I'd seen them. The badge on her lapel confirmed my suspicions. 'AoM', it read. This was the grey government lady in a different guise and instantly I knew I'd not return home that day. Or any other day. I took the letter from her and spied my mother's elegant penmanship. Raising it to my nose, I breathed in her scent and closed my eyes. When I opened them again, the 'Angel of Mercy' had left our carriage and moved onto the next.

"I'd heard of these rescue missions before, having overheard my parents' whispered conversations when I was supposed to be sleeping. I didn't read my letter until later. My classmates cried, yelled and screamed around me. But I remained quite still, staring at the endless greenery as the train chugged up the mountainside, a mild drizzle now spraying its fine mist upon those close to the edge.

"My parents were saving me from the harshness of impending war, sending me to safety so that I might survive the evil times that we lived in. I was alone, but knew they'd done this out of love. I owed it to them - and to the Angels of Mercy who made it all possible - to be the best boy and ultimately the best man I could. I would keep that promise."

Valerie wiped a tear from her cheek. Many seated before her mirrored the action, also moved by Eric's tender words. A moment or so passed until she felt able to continue. "I don't recall meeting my Cousin Eric; I was but a child when he visited us. My own father," she gestured to a silver-haired man sitting in the front row, "told me Eric was a gentle soul. Quiet, unassuming and modest. As you all know, the reason I'm here today, reading from his notes, is because dear Cousin Eric bequeathed me this building and the business he had so lovingly built up. It was his wish that I, or rather," she stretched out her arms to encompass everyone, "we continue his legacy and entrust that every child who enters here shall be as loved as he was."

The audience clapped and cheered. Valerie's father stood and joined her on the raised platform. "If I may say a few words?"

Valerie stepped back, smiling. "Please do."

"Eric never talked much about his childhood at all. He was an academic, his nose always in a book. As we see, his endeavours paid off. He opened this orphanage twenty years ago and has - I'm sure you'll agree - been a most generous benefactor and, indeed, host to many hundreds of children." A sea of nodding heads echoed the sentiment as a group of youngsters, aged between seven and thirteen, entered the room, carrying trays of soft drinks and juice in paper cups. They offered the drinks to everyone in the room, then took their own and sat cross-legged on the floor. "Eric wrote these notes many years after the atrocities, having been approached by a reporter to tell his story. The tale was never published. Whether from shyness or to remain private, he withdrew from the agreement and buried the memories in a safe place away from prying and pitiful eyes. Only now have we, his family, learnt of these details, and we thought it apt to share them with you, Eric's own Angels. So, if you'll excuse the glassware, please join me in a toast." He waited while everyone stood, the children included and then raised his own cup. "To Eric and the Angels of Mercy Orphanage."

"To Cousin Eric," said Valerie, after everyone had returned the toast, "and may every child be as loved."

New Beginnings by Brook Dean

TOWARDS THE SUN

Where'er you may go and where'er you are from
Spread your wings and fly towards the sun.

Whate'er you may be and whate'er you might become
Spread your wings and fly towards the sun.

-T. M. Lowe

Towards the Sun by T. M. Lowe

TINFOIL HEART

We create when we are happy

We create when we are lonely

We create tinfoil hearts

With our hands

God why did you create me

I feel close to you as I am forming

In your mind

Please understand &

Don't tear apart

My tinfoil heart

-Deanna Stinson

WHERE HOPE IS

Wherever something grows
There is hope

For from the shackles
Was freedom found

Awaken to a new dawn
Where each day is magic

The nectar of the Eternal
Filling every crevice
Of your being

The light of the Infinite
Reaching into each molecule
Of your mind

The knowledge of love
Nestling in your soul

Hope flourishes here
Grows in strength here

It breathes
And lives

In you
In me
In all

-Adrienne T. Nugent

SOARING

Standing on the edge of the mountain cliff,
Looking far out, my vision can't believe this,
The vast drop below, I couldn't perceive it,
The fear in my head for a second makes my mind drift,
But I'm going on anyway, it's just superfluous,
To let an obstacle stand in my way, this is my confidence.

So I backpedal to grant myself some distance,
Prepare my heart to take on the task I envisioned,
And with my stubbornness inside I'm commissioned,
Taking off running with ever proficient precision,
Speeding up, ready to take to the air, no collisions,
Leaping off the ledge, mentally high on my ambitions!

And it hits me, that now I've really done it,
Jumping off of the ground as I was gunning,
Nothing beneath me and now my thoughts are running,
The faith of all those placed in me, it has been stunning,
Only now does the knot form in my stomach, my heart is racing,
This is a whole new path, world, adventure I am facing!

Towards the Sun

As I start to descend, my thoughts start coming in,
It's time for me to finally open fully my wings again,
Just like that, things become completely wild,
I begin to ascend, feeling lighter than all the clouds,
Itonami filling my lungs, my eyes open proud,
Reinvigorated and smiling, I am screaming loud.

I wouldn't believed that I could have reached this far,
But I have grown and been cared for, for this, I am strong,
Any challenge, any struggle now I will come to head on,
As I feel this wind, this pressure that uplifts under my wings,
Reminding me of the first time I launched myself off a swing,
The rushing, the feeling of the air, it all emboldens me.

The pause while you are so high, the slow down of all time,
Your perception then becomes controlled by your higher mind,
Giving you a chance to see what you may not have noticed,
Taking in everything around as your mind blooms like a lotus,
When the excitement hits, this is what will take your focus,
As all it speeds by while you leave behind these beautiful moments.

I'll take all of that, enjoy it all to its fullest,
As the cold air reawakens me at my coolest,
For those who support my growth already knew this,
For empowering me and seeing me charging right through this,
Their belief in me, that they've given me, that's my best gift,
And with it, from my purpose I will never let myself drift.

Soaring

As I fly above the clouds, looking down and absorbing the sites,

Crossing over the twilight as the day becomes the night,

Adjusting my eyes, staring at the captivating blinking lights,

Catching glimpses of movement beneath the glow tonight,

As I make my descent with an earnest, happy intent,

Coming down to rest my wings, my stamina almost spent.

I see the landing zone in front, encircled in gleaming sparks,

And closing in I am finding hopeful eyes at my mark,

The people that stood behind me and gave me my start,

As I prepare to touch down, they rush towards me in a hurry,

And when I land they wrap around me, tightening but no worry,

I take the moment to embrace them all, their love strengthens me wholly.

-Andre Ratchford

Monday Motivation #114 by Kévin Jean-Philippe

TEMPLE

I am a temple made for a holy spirit

A vase filled with many dreams

That pour out like water

To form the mist upon my wings

-Deanna Stinson

GRATITUDE

And I am
Reminded of love
Each time
The sparrow sings

The sun showering
Its rays
The peace
Its magic brings

For in
Each moment
Is a miracle

A chance
To glance

To feel
To breathe
In

Everything

-Adrienne T. Nugent

WHISPERS

Whispers
All around
All knowing
All seeing
All hearing
They know your heart
They've heard your cries
They've touched your soul

Whispers
You may have heard them
They hope you have
They speak to you
They speak to me
They speak to all
But life
Life has drowned them out

Whispers
They bring good news
They bring good memories
They bring good feelings
If only you listen

Whispers
All around
All knowing
All seeing
All hearing
All for you

-K.N. Nguyen

WHITE MAGE

Stars fall down in a spiral motion

Turning to stone like pillars in the ocean

Tides splash all around me it

Sounds like a full moon melody

And I hear songs like

Words of eternity

Return to me

God is like a white mage

Who bathes my soul in prisms of smoke and sage

-Deanna Stinson

I Am

I am strength

I am resilience

I am the hope that turns darkness to light

I am courage

I am freedom

I am faith that holds everything safe in my arms

I am eternal

I am unlimited

I am the harmony that keeps the universe balanced

I am

-K.N. Nguyen

ENCHANTED MOON

Your heart is like a mirror and I am the seer of love

Words rise up from my lips

I can feel the sun kiss me

I am never alone

Your anger is like a natural disaster

I put the beast to sleep with a song

My halo is a divine flower growing from a seed

I nourish with powerful thoughts

Our souls are like vines twisting

Nurtured in green gardens of the underworld

Dreams pour from the moon and slip through my hands like memories

-Deanna Stinson

New Adventures by Emma Cepeda

ABOUT ANTHONY AMUNDSON

A software engineer by trade, Anthony has been writing since grade school. He loves both science fiction and science fact. He is also an astronomer, computer gamer, rockhound, jeweler, and gardener. He currently lives in Minnesota with his wife.

ABOUT EMMA CEPEDA

Her work can be found on Instagram under the name @artbyenc

ABOUT BROOK DEAN

Brook Dean is a 48-year-old self-taught artist who is still studying in the "School of Hard Knocks." Originally from California, he has lived in Florida off and on since 1982. He has been residing in St. Augustine, Florida, since 2006 with his three children and wife of 20 years. His passions include surfing, skateboarding, and cats.

You can find more artwork from Brook Dean on Instagram at @shredtat; he also works as a tattoo artist at Stay True Tattoo on 199 West King Street in St. Augustine, Florida.

ABOUT LS FELLOWS

Despite being born in Britain, her heart now lies in Spain. Many moons ago, she was a student in Granada, Spain, a place she adores to this day. Back then, she swore she'd return one day on a more permanent basis. In 2003, she did just that. Now, as a translator and fur-mum to two adorable but mischievous mutts, in her free time she can usually be spotted with her nose in a book, armed with just the teeniest chunk of chocolate and a zillion pomegranates! If she's not reading, she'll be writing … or eating chocolate and pomegranates. She also writes as bea kendall (mysteries and suspense) and maye palmer (women's and historical fiction).

ABOUT KÉVIN JEAN-PHILIPPE

Kévin is a 2D/3D artist with Advenworks intent on living The Artlife™ who hails from Guadeloupe in the Caribbean. He knew early on that he wanted to draw characters for video games and manga. Then he found out "character artist" was an actual job when he downloaded the Art Book for Final Fantasy 9; the rest is history. His previous work includes Slashrun and Snake Blast, both available on iOS and Android.

You can find his ongoing art series Monday Motivation posts via Instagram (@theCluelessArtist).

ABOUT ESTEE LEE-MOUNTEL

Estee began writing professionally as a journalist with campus publica-tions and Sacramento News & Review, creating narrative nonfiction and feature pieces. Now, by day, she is a quasi-librarian (or "library services assistant," according to the HR Department) for the Public Library of Cincinnati and Hamilton County. By night, however, she transforms into a writer and artist. She is part of the publishing group DragonScript as a writer and editor; her short stories can be found in their two anthologies New Beginnings and New Adventures.

Estee is also the lead writer and editor for indie mobile game company Advenworks, headquartered in Paris, France. Her previous works include Birdy Party and Slashrun. She launched her first major interactive fiction title, Loop: The Distress Call, in March of 2020 for iOS and Android. (For more information, visit advenworks.com/loop-the-distress-call.)

She's a native Californian currently living in Cincinnati, Ohio with her husband, the Orc, and their two kids, the Whelpling and the Broodling. If she isn't writing, drawing, saving the world/galaxy in a video game, or juggling a million tasks as a working mom, she's probably baking up something sweet.

You can still follow her oft-punny and nerdy musings on Twitter @Toriah_the_Mom.

About T. M. Lowe

T. M. Lowe was an aspiring writer from Jacksonville, Florida, when her mother took her own life in 2012. Mrs. Lowe stopped following her life-long passion while trying to figure out how to cope with the sudden, unexpected loss. Four years later, she determined to take up writing again in her mother's memory.

Her first published works were "What Makes a Man", a science fiction short story and "The Lady and the Dragon", a fantasy short story. Both appeared in DragonScript's first anthology, New Beginnings.

In DragonScript's second anthology, New Adventures, she contributed "Dead Land", a science fiction short story and "The Lady and the Hunter", a fantasy short story sequel to "The Lady and the Dragon". She is currently working on more short stories as well as a full-length novel.

Mrs. Lowe is 35 years old and currently resides in St. Augustine, Florida, with her husband and household of rescued animals. When not writing, her hobbies include playing video games, watching her beloved Florida Gators play football in the fall, reading, attending medieval and renaissance faires in full knightly costume, fishing, and shooting pool while drinking whiskey in smoky dive bars.

To catch updates on her current writing projects, follow her on Twitter at @TiffanyMLowe or visit her Facebook page at facebook.com/AuthorTMLowe.

About K.N. Nguyen

K.N. Nguyen is a fantasy author and the founder of DragonScript, a group that offers an outlet for new writers. Growing up, she often found herself immersed in some imaginary world, conquering enemy nations, and saving the day. As time went on, her love for horrible puns and nerd culture pulled her out of these worlds and brought her back to reality.

It wasn't until she started working at her office job that she felt the itch to begin writing. Her debut novel, King's Blood, was released in 2018. It is the first of a high fantasy series drawing on her love of ancient Mediterranean mythology and epic fantasy.

A native of Sacramento, California, K.N. Nguyen spends her time singing karaoke, playing taiko, enjoying rhythm dancing games, and travelling with her friends and family when she isn't writing.

You can find her on Facebook at facebook.com/AuthorKNNguyen or at dragonscript.net

ABOUT ADRIENNE T. NUGENT

Adrienne T. Nugent is a Canadian-born writer and gamer who has always been fascinated by magical worlds, fantastical characters, and the books they can be found in. Hoping to spread love and diversity through writing, she's currently working on setting the myriad of stories she has in her head loose upon the world. You can find her on Twitter at @miryoku7 and read even more of her unique thoughts at miryoku7.tumblr.com

About Joseph Piliero

Joe is an award-winning graphic designer and former design manager in New York City's publishing world. His passions include an obsessive interest in Latin, Italian Renaissance, and outer space. Joe is also a crazy-obsessive amateur baker, researching history behind recipes and chemistry of ingredients. Online portfolio and contact info: behance.net/jpiliero.

ABOUT ANDRE RATCHFORD

Growing up, Andre was always a dreamer and spent a great deal of his youth writing and creating his own worlds and characters. This stemmed from his love of video games, cartoons and comic books. He even ventured into poetry in his teens and still continues to work creatively to this day, having and continuing to publish his own books. However, his creativity doesn't end there, Andre runs a YouTube Channel under the moniker "The Game Idea Guy" where he talks about his own ideas for video games as well as many subjects related to gaming in general. He also is co-host to a weekly podcast dubbed "Wingin IT" with his partner in crime, Jay Flemming on the "Geek Life" channel to talk about current events in gaming/geek culture or whatever on the spot subject they come up with. Andre will continue to work on and improve his creative endeavors into varying styles of content for the world.

The Game Idea Guy YouTube Channel Link:
https://www.youtube.com/channel/UCKL6qh5mFk5YDmK4xpxxlEg

The Geek Life YouTube Channel Link:
https://www.youtube.com/user/jeremiah2607

Andre Ratchford Amazon Author Profile:
https://www.amazon.com/Andre-Ratchford/e/B085PQBY9Q/

The Game Idea Guy Twitter:
https://twitter.com/GVGINU

ABOUT DEANNA STINSON

A native of California, Deanna is an artist and an award-winning poet. She is a college-trained entrepreneur and a Costa Rican Times writer. Self-described as a lightworker, medium, musician, Pagan vegetarian. She can be followed on Twitter under @wishthegreatest and her portfolio is viewable at teardropsofanangel.com

ABOUT MEL TONG

Mel is a writer with interests all over the board, but one thing has stayed constant: her love to escape reality with some great fantasy world. It's helped keep the kid in her alive. She has a BS degree in Chemical Engineering and an MS degree in Molecular Pharmacology and Toxicology.

www.ingramcontent.com/pod-product-compliance
Lightning Source LLC
Chambersburg PA
CBHW060804210726
48292CB00013B/1750